*a min**e**dition book*

North American edition published 2014 by Michael Neugebauer Publishing Ltd. Hong Kong

Illustrations copyright © 2014 by Yana Sedova
Original title: Snedronningen
English text translation by Anthea Bell
Rights arranged with "minedition" Rights and Licensing AG, Zurich, Switzerland.

Michael Neugebauer Publishing Ltd., Unit 23, 7F, Kowloon Bay Industrial Centre,
15 Wang Hoi Road, Kowloon Bay, Hong Kong.
e-mail: info@minedition.com
This book was printed in July 2014 at Beijing AF printing. Opto-Mechatronics Industrial
Park No.2, ZhengFu Road, Tong Zhou District, Beijing, China
Typesetting in Tiffany ItcT
Color separation by Pixelstorm, Vienna
Library of Congress Cataloging-in-Publication Data available upon request.

ISBN 978-988-8240-78-4

10 9 8 7 6 5 4 3 2 1
First Impression

For more information please visit our website: www.minedition.com

Hans Christian Andersen

The Snow Queen

A Tale in Seven Stories

with Pictures by Yana Sedova

retold by Anthea Bell

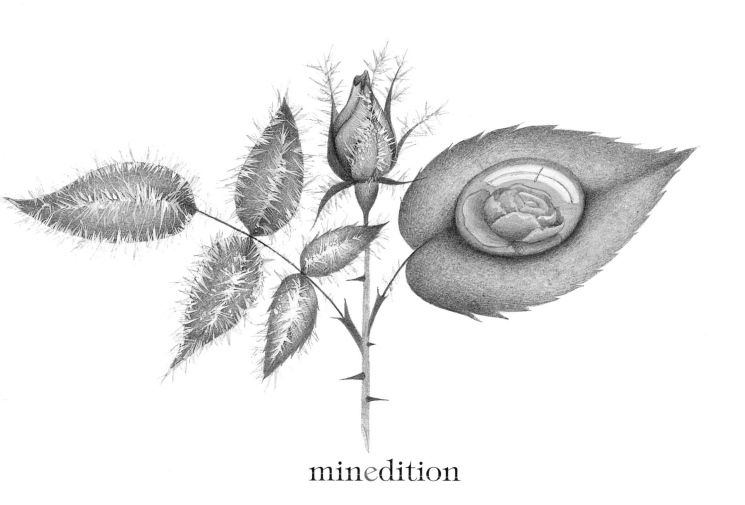

minedition

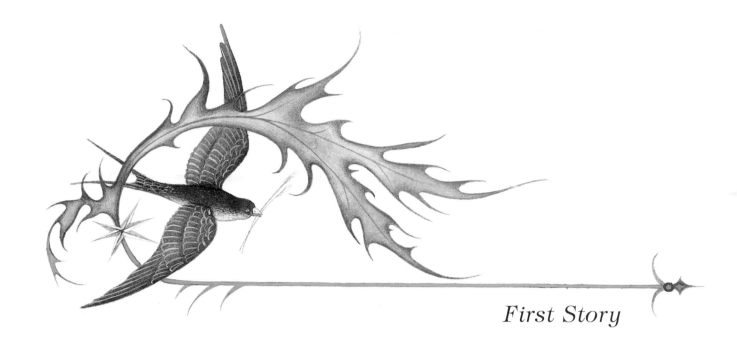

THE FRAGMENTS OF A MIRROR

This tale begins with a wicked goblin, one of the very worst – you might call him the devil in person. One day, when he was in a good temper, he made a mirror, and anything his mirror reflected that was good and beautiful shrank to almost nothing. However, it made all that was bad and ugly seem far larger than it really was. The mirror made lovely landscapes look like boiled spinach, and however attractive people were in real life, they looked hideously distorted in the mirror.

The devil was highly amused by his distorting mirror, which could even reflect thoughts, but not truthfully. It showed good thoughts as bad impulses, and the devil liked that very much.
As it happened, the devil ran a school, and all his students agreed that the mirror was a wonderful invention. For the first time, they claimed, the world and all its people could be seen as they really were.

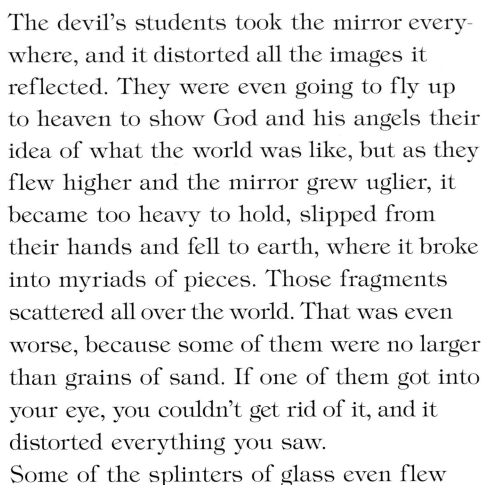

The devil's students took the mirror everywhere, and it distorted all the images it reflected. They were even going to fly up to heaven to show God and his angels their idea of what the world was like, but as they flew higher and the mirror grew uglier, it became too heavy to hold, slipped from their hands and fell to earth, where it broke into myriads of pieces. Those fragments scattered all over the world. That was even worse, because some of them were no larger than grains of sand. If one of them got into your eye, you couldn't get rid of it, and it distorted everything you saw.

Some of the splinters of glass even flew into people's hearts, turning them as hard and cold as ice. Others were large enough for window panes, and you wouldn't have wanted to see your friends through those windows. Smaller fragments of the mirror could be made into eye-glasses, and people who wore them could no longer tell right from wrong.

The devil was delighted, and laughed and laughed. There are still some fragments of that wicked glass in the air, and this is the story of what two of them did.

A Little Boy and a Little Girl

The city was so full of buildings that few people could have gardens, but two poor children, a little boy called Kay and a little girl called Gerda, had the next best thing. They lived opposite each other in the attics of two houses with a gutter running between them. Their parents grew herbs in wooden boxes at the attic windows, and a rose bush in each box. The children were great friends, and in the summer they could sit out by the window-boxes and play together.

In winter, when the windows often froze over, Kay and Gerda heated up copper pennies and melted peepholes on the windows with them, so that they could see each other. And if they ran up and down the stairs of their two houses, they could still play indoors.

One day, when thick snowflakes were swirling in the air outside the windows, Gerda's grandmother asked the children, "Look, do you see the white bees swarming?"

"Oh yes," said Kay. "Do they have a
queen, like the real bees in summer?"
"To be sure," said Grandmother.
"The Snow Queen flies among
the thickest of the snowflakes,
and never comes down to earth
at all, but goes back to the dark
snow clouds."
"On winter nights, she flies through
the streets, looks in at the windows
and leaves frost-flowers on them."
"We've seen those," said little Kay
and Gerda, so they knew it was true.
"Can the Snow Queen get indoors?"
asked Gerda.

"If she does," said Kay, "I'll melt her on the stove."
But Grandmother went on to tell them other stories.
That evening, when Kay was going to bed, he looked out of the
window. A few snowflakes were still falling, and a large one
settled on one of the window-boxes. It grew and grew until it
became a woman in a gauzy white gown of star-shaped flakes.
She was the Snow Queen, and she was very beautiful, made all
of glittering ice with eyes that sparkled like stars, though there
was no peace or kindness in them. She nodded and waved to
Kay. He was afraid, and thought he saw a large bird flying past
the window.

The next day dawned cold and clear, but soon the snow melted and spring came, with sunlight, and green grass growing. Kay and Gerda could play in their garden on the roof, and the roses blossomed beautifully that year. Gerda had learned a psalm with roses in it, and the children sang it together.

Roses wither where they lie,
But God's dear love will never die.

That was a wonderful summer for little Kay and Gerda. But one day, as they sat in the sun looking at a picture-book while the church clock struck five, Kay cried out, "Oh, something hurts my heart! And some dust has flown into my eye."

Gerda looked for the dust, but seeing nothing, she said, "I think it's gone away." However, it had not. One of those fragments of the devil's mirror had flown into Kay's eye, and a splinter of the magic glass had pierced his heart. "Why are you crying?" he asked Gerda. "It makes you so ugly, and I'm all right now." And then, as his heart began turning to ice, he cried, "Oh, look at that ugly, worm-eaten rose - and this one is crooked as well!" With those words he kicked the window boxes, tore off the roses and ran away, leaving Gerda alone.

The next time Gerda wanted to look at the picture book, Kay said it was silly and just for babies. He teased Gerda and made fun of Grandmother and her stories.

When winter came again, with the first snow, he looked at the structure of the snowflakes through a magnifying glass. "See these snowflakes," he told Gerda. "They're perfect, and much more beautiful than real live flowers."

One day Kay and the other boys took their little sleighs out to the city square, where they tied them to the farmers' carts arriving from the country and hitched a free ride. Kay tied his to a huge, white sleigh, driven by someone in a shaggy white fur cloak and cap. The sleigh went faster and faster, the driver turned and nodded to Kay, and he found that he couldn't get loose again. On and on went the big sleigh and the little one. Kay felt that they were flying like the wind over hedges and ditches. He was scared, but when he tried to say his prayers, all he could think of was the multiplication tables.

When at last the big sleigh stopped among snowflakes falling so densely they looked like big white chickens, the driver stood up, and he recognized the Snow Queen.

"What a fine drive that was!" she said. "But you're trembling – come into my fur cloak." She wrapped it around him, and it felt like sinking into a snowdrift. "Are you still cold?" asked the Queen, kissing his forehead. That kiss was deathly cold, cold as the ice that was already in his heart. For a moment he thought he was dying, but soon he was used to the cold, and he saw that his sleigh was tied to one of the big white snowflakes flying along with them. And when the Snow Queen kissed Kay again he forgot Gerda's grandmother, his home, and little Gerda.

"But no more kisses now, or I shall kiss you to death," said the Snow Queen. Kay told her all the clever things he knew - arithmetic and geography - and she kept smiling. They rode on and on through the air and over the clouds, and the storm seemed to be singing old songs.

Over lakes and forests Kay flew with the Snow Queen, over land and over sea as the wild wind blew, wolves howled, crows cawed and the snow crackled. Above them shone the great, clear moon. Kay watched it all night long, and when day dawned he slept at the Snow Queen's feet.

THE WOMAN WHO WORKED MAGIC AND HER FLOWER GARDEN

What about little Gerda, now that her friend Kay had gone? No one knew what had happened to him. Even the other boys could say only that he had hitched his little sleigh to a big one, and they had driven out of town. Gerda shed bitter tears, thinking that Kay must be dead, drowned in the nearby river, and when spring came, she said, "My friend Kay is dead and gone."

"I don't believe it," said the sun.

"Kay is dead and gone," she told the swallows.

"We don't believe it either,"
they said, and in the end Gerda
wasn't sure whether she herself
believed it or not. Early one
morning she decided to put on her
new red shoes and try to find out
where Kay was.

When she came to the river, she asked,
"Have you taken my friend Kay away?
If you'll give him back, you can have my red
shoes."

She thought the ripples were nodding, so she
threw her shoes into the water, but not far
enough, because the water carried them back
to land. There was a boat near the bank, and
Gerda got into it to throw the shoes further
out. But the boat wasn't tied up, so it drifted
away, taking Gerda with it, and her red shoes
floated after her.

The river banks were very pretty, with flowers and old trees
growing on them, and a pasture where cattle and sheep grazed,
but there wasn't a human soul in sight. Perhaps the river is taking
me to Kay, thought Gerda, and she cheered up. At last the boat
brought her to a cherry orchard with two soldiers outside a little
red house, presenting arms. Gerda called to them, but then she
saw that they were mechanical wooden figures.

She called louder as the boat drifted closer to the bank, and an old woman leaning on a stick came out of her house. She was wearing a big sun hat painted with beautiful flowers.

"Poor child," said the old woman to Gerda. "How did you get here on the fast-flowing river?" Then she walked into the water, drew the boat to land with her stick, and helped Gerda out. Although she was rather frightened of the old woman, Gerda was glad to be back on land.

The old woman asked how she came to be there, and Gerda told her story. "Have you seen my friend Kay?" she asked. The old woman said no, but he might yet arrive, and she invited Gerda to eat cherries and look at her flowers, which all had stories to tell. Then she took Gerda indoors, gave her some cherries, combed her hair with a golden comb, and asked her to stay for a while. Now this old woman could work magic. She was not a wicked witch, but she wanted to keep Gerda with her, and guessing that the rose bushes in her garden would remind Gerda of Kay, she cast a spell to send them down into the ground, and keep the little girl from going in search of him again.

Then the old woman took Gerda into her lovely, scented garden. The best flowers of every season of the year bloomed in that garden all at once, and Gerda played with them until the sun set behind the cherry trees. Then she slept in a bed with a red silk quilt embroidered with violets, and she had dreams as happy as a queen might dream on her wedding day.

This went on for many days. Gerda came to know all the flowers very well, yet she always felt there was something missing. One day, however, as she looked at the old woman's sun hat, she saw the picture of a rose on it, and knew what the missing flower was. When the old woman had sent the real rose bushes down to hide underground, she had forgotten about the rose on her hat.

"Aren't there any roses in this garden?" asked Gerda.

She went searching the garden, and when she couldn't find a rose at all she sat down and cried. But it so happened that her hot tears fell just where one of the rose bushes had sunk into the ground, and when the bush felt her tears, it grew again as lovely as ever.

Then she remembered the roses at home in the city, and her dear friend little Kay.

"Oh, I've waited here too long," cried Gerda. "I forgot to look for Kay. Do you know where he is? Do you think he's dead and gone?"

"No," said the roses. "We have been down in the ground where the dead people go, and he wasn't there."

Then Gerda asked the other flowers if they had seen Kay, but each flower knew only its own story. Although they told Gerda those stories, she heard nothing about her friend Kay.

What did the tiger lily say? "Do you hear the drum go boom-boom? Just two notes all the time. Do you hear the women lamenting and the priests chanting? A Hindu woman stands by her dead husband's funeral pyre. The flames are rising to burn them both, but she thinks of the eyes of a living man that burn even hotter. Can the flames of the heart die in the fire?"

"I'm afraid I don't understand that story," said Gerda.

"Well, it's my tale," said the tiger lily.

What did the convolvulus say? "I see a castle in the mountains, on a narrow path. Ivy grows up to the balcony where a fair maiden stands looking down the road. She is as graceful as a rose, as delicate as an apple blossom. 'Is he never coming?' she sighs."

"Do you mean Kay?" asked Gerda.

"That's the story I dream," said the convolvulus.

What did the snowdrop say?

"I see a swing hanging in the trees, with two little girls in white dresses on it. Their brother, a bigger boy, is standing on the swing, holding the ropes with his arms. He has a cup of soapy water in one hand and a bubble pipe in the other, and a black dog is barking at the children, but the swing won't stop. Then the bubble bursts, and that's my story."

"Very pretty too, but it sounds sad, and you didn't mention Kay," said Gerda.

What did the hyacinths say?

"There were three fair, translucent sisters,
one in a red dress, the second in a blue dress,
the third dressed all in white.
They danced hand in hand in the moonlight beside
a lake, but they were humans and not fairy folk.
The fragrance was sweet as the sisters went on
into the forest, and the air smelled sweeter still.
Then the sisters' caskets came gliding out of the
trees and across the lake. Are the sisters asleep or
dead? The fragrant flowers say they are dead, and
we ring their death knell."

"What a sad story," said Gerda. "Is Kay dead after
all, then? The roses were down in the earth,
and they said he wasn't."

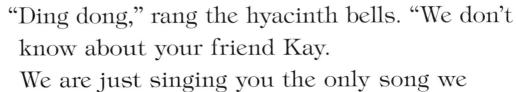

"Ding dong," rang the hyacinth bells. "We don't know about your friend Kay.

We are just singing you the only song we know."

Then Gerda went to see the buttercup, gleaming gold among its bright green leaves.

"Oh," said Gerda, "you're as bright as the sun. Do you know where I can find my friend Kay?"

The buttercup certainly shone brightly, but what song would it sing? Not a song about Kay. "The sun shone on the first day of spring," said the buttercup. "It shone on the white wall next door, where the spring flowers were yellow in the sunlight. A grandmother sat at the door in her chair, and her granddaughter, a poor but pretty maidservant, had come to visit the old lady. There was gold in the kiss she gave her grandmother, a golden heart in the girl, it was a golden morning, and that's my story done," said the buttercup.

"My poor dear grandmother," said Gerda. "How she must miss me, and Kay as well. But we'll soon both be home. I'm tired of the flowers' stories. They never tell me anything useful."

And she was tucking up her skirt
to run faster, but then a narcissus
brushed against her leg, and she
bent down.

"What can you tell me?" she asked.
So what did the narcissus say?
"I can see myself! Oh, I smell so
sweet! A little dancer, half
dressed, is standing in the attic.
She is only an illusion. She pours
water from the teapot on a bodice
she is holding, because cleanliness
is next to godliness.

Her white dress is on a hanger, she has a saffron scarf around
her neck. 'I can see myself!' she repeats. 'I can see myself!'"

"Who cares?" said Gerda, and running to the end of the garden,
she managed to unlatch the gate, and went out barefoot. She
looked back, but no one was following her, and on looking around
she saw that summer was over.

She would never have guessed that in the old woman's magic
flower garden.

Oh, thought Gerda, I've wasted so much time.

She was tired, her feet were sore, and everywhere she looked it
was cold and dismal. The willow leaves were yellow, there were
still berries on the blackthorn, but they tasted sour. The whole
wide world seemed so dark and weary now.

THE PRINCE AND THE PRINCESS

When Gerda had to stop for a rest, she saw a big crow hopping over the snow. "Caw, caw!" he said, and although he didn't speak a human language very well he did his best. He asked Gerda where she was going all alone.

So she told him the whole sad story, and asked whether by any chance he had seen Kay.

"Maybe I have," cawed the crow. "Maybe I have."

Gerda hugged the crow hard. "Oh, do you really think so?" she asked.

"Take it easy!" said the bird. "It could have been Kay that I saw, but if so then he will have forgotten you for the sake of the princess."

"Is he living with a princess?" asked poor Gerda, dismayed.

"Whether or not your friend is now the prince I can't be sure, but I'll tell you all I know. The princess of this country is very clever - so clever that she's read all the newspapers in the world and has forgotten them again. She was sitting on her throne one day when a song came into her head. It had a refrain that went, 'Why wouldn't I get married today, married today, married today?'

"'Well, why not?' said the princess to herself, and she decided to marry any man who would talk to her sensibly, and not just look handsome. She called her ladies in waiting together, and they all agreed that it was a good idea. And you can rely on every word I say," added the crow, "because I am engaged to marry my tame girlfriend who lives in the palace, so I have it from the crow's mouth. It was announced that the princess would marry any young man who could hold a good conversation with her, and young men came in crowds. They could talk well enough outside the palace, but once they were in such grand surroundings all their talk dried up, and when they faced the princess they could only repeat the last thing she herself had said, which was no fun for her at all. So she didn't choose a husband on the first day, or the second day either."

"But when did Kay arrive?" asked Gerda. "Was he one of those young men?"

"Take it easy!" said the crow again. "I'm coming to that. On the third day a young fellow with bright eyes like yours turned up. He didn't come with a horse and carriage, his clothes were shabby, and his boots creaked terribly ..."

"Oh," cried Gerda, "that must have been Kay! He had new boots, and they really did creak! I heard them in Grandmother's room!"

"They certainly creaked," said the crow, "but he didn't let that or the grandeur of the palace bother him. He went straight up to the princess, who was sitting on a pearl as big as a spinning wheel, surrounded by her ladies and gentlemen in waiting."

"How alarming!" said Gerda. "But did the princess win Kay's heart?"

"She'd have won mine if I wasn't a crow, with a girlfriend of my own," said the bird. "And my girlfriend the tame crow saw the whole scene, so you may believe what I say. The young man told the princess that he hadn't come to try to impress her, but to hear what wise things she herself had to say, and they had such an enjoyable conversation that they fell in love with each other at once."

"Oh yes, that was Kay," said Gerda. "He's so clever that he can even do fractions. Please will you take me to the palace to see him?"

"That's easier said than done," said the crow. "But I'll see whether my tame girlfriend can help you. Wait for me here," he said, and he flew away.

When he came back it was dark, and he was carrying a nice bread roll in his beak, "Caw, caw, this is for you," he said. "My girlfriend thinks you must be hungry. She says the guards in their silver uniforms wouldn't let you into the front of the palace, barefoot as you are, but she knows where to find the key to a little back staircase, and we will take you up to the royal bedroom that way."

So Gerda and the crow went up the back stairs. Gerda was both afraid and glad of the chance of seeing Kay again, even if he had married the princess. She hoped that at least he, too, would be glad to see her, and hear about all her adventures on the way, and when she met the crow's tame girlfriend, who was perched beside a small lamp, she curtseyed politely.

"My friend here has told me your story," said the tame crow, "and it has touched our hearts. Please carry that lamp, so that we can see our way upstairs."

"Isn't that someone I can hear on the stairs?"

asked Gerda, for she thought she saw the shadows of ladies and gentlemen on horseback coming up behind them and racing along the walls.

"Those are dreams," said the tame crow, "taking the minds of the prince and princess out hunting. You will have a good chance of seeing them asleep now – and we hope that if they show you favor tomorrow, you will be grateful to us crows."

"I am sure she will," said the crow whom Gerda had first met. "Gerda is a grateful girl."

The crows took Gerda into another room with draperies of rose satin, embroidered with flowers, and here again the shadowy dreams rode past. They went on from room to magnificent room, and at last came to the royal bedroom, which had a ceiling like a palm-tree with leaves of precious crystal glass. Two beds like lilies, one white and one red, hung from a great golden stem. The princess was asleep in the white bed, and Gerda, hoping to find Kay in the red one, folded back a red petal and saw a little brown neck. Feeling sure it was Kay, she called out his name and held up the lamp she was carrying.

The dreams chased back into the room, and he woke – but only his neck was like Kay's, not the handsome young prince's face. Gerda's voice woke the princess, who sat up and asked what the matter was.
So she told her story.

"You poor, dear girl," said the kind prince and princess. They weren't cross with the crows for bringing her into the palace, and promised that if they liked they could be Court Crows for life, with first choice of scraps from the royal kitchen.

The crows were overjoyed to accept the offer.
The prince gave up his bed to Gerda, so that
she could rest, and as she slept, thinking how
kind the crows and the royal couple alike were, the
dreams came back. This time she saw little Kay in a
dream – the dream was like an angel pulling him along
in his sleigh. But when she woke up, the dream was gone.
Now Gerda was dressed in silk and velvet, and invited to
stay in the palace, but she said she wanted to go on in search
of Kay. So she was given boots and a warm muff, and the prince
and princess gave her a golden carriage with a coachman, a footman, and outriders.

The prince and princess helped Gerda into the carriage, wishing her good luck, and the crows came to see her off as well. They had just been married, and the tame crow had a headache brought on by over-eating, but her husband went the first few miles with Gerda. The carriage itself had plenty of sweet cakes, fruit and gingerbread for Gerda to eat. She had already said goodbye to the prince and princess, and the tame crow, and when her friend the other crow flew back to join his wife it was a sad goodbye.

Fifth Story

THE LITTLE ROBBER GIRL

The carriage drove on into a dark forest, where its gleaming gold caught the eyes of some robbers.

They weren't going to let such a treasure pass.

"Look, gold, gold!" they cried. They seized the horses, killed the coachman, footman and outriders, and dragged Gerda out of the carriage.

"Oh, doesn't she look tender and plump," said the old robber woman who had a beard and bristly eyebrows. "This little girl will taste good!" And she brought out a sharp, shiny knife.

But then she screamed, "Ouch!" Because she was carrying her daughter on her back, and the little robber girl had bitten her mother's ear. That saved Gerda's life.

"Oh no, you don't," said the little robber girl. "She's my friend, she must give me her muff and her pretty dress, and we'll share the same bed." Then she bit her mother again, and all the robbers laughed at the sight.

"I want a ride in the carriage," said the little robber girl, and she and Gerda got into it and drove away into the heart of the forest.

The little robber girl was about Gerda's own size, but
stronger and black-eyed. She hugged Gerda and said,
"I won't let the robbers kill you unless you make me cross
with you. Are you a princess?"
"No," said Gerda, and she told her story, and said she
was looking for her friend little Kay.
The robber girl nodded, and said, "Even if you do make
me cross, they won't kill you, because I'll do it myself."
Then she took Gerda's muff away for her own, but at
least she dried her new friend's eyes first.
The carriage stopped when they came to the robbers'
castle, where ravens and crows flew in and out, and huge
bulldogs leaped up in the air, but they were not allowed
to bark.

There was a fire burning in the middle of the hall, which had no chimney, so that the smoke had to make its way out of a hole in the roof. There was a big pan of soup boiling over the fire, with rabbits and hares roasting on the spit. "You can sleep with me and my little pet animals tonight," said the little robber girl, when they had had some supper, and she took Gerda to a corner of the hall where a hundred doves were roosting on the rafters overhead. "These are mine," she told Gerda, picking up a dove and pushing it into Gerda's face. "Up in that cage there are two wood-pigeons. And here's another old friend of mine."

With those words she dragged a reindeer tied by a chain to a copper ring out of his cage, took a knife out of a chink in the wall, and stroked the poor animal's neck with it. Then she made Gerda lie down beside her.

"Are you going to sleep with that knife beside you?" asked Gerda.

"I always sleep with it, just in case I need it," said the little robber girl. "But now tell me your story about little Kay again."

So Gerda told the story. The wood-pigeons cooed, the doves slept, and so did the little robber girl, while the robbers drank and sang by the fire.

Then the wood-pigeons said, "Coo, coo, we saw little Kay, we two! He flew in the Snow Queen's sleigh, as she blew on the nest where we lay. The baby birds died, all but we two – coo, coo, coo."

"What did you say?" asked Gerda. "Do you know where the Snow Queen was going?"

"Very likely to Lapland," said the wood-pigeons. "There's always snow and ice there – ask that reindeer beside you. Coo, coo, coo."

"Yes, that's true, true, true," said the reindeer. "You can gallop over those sparkling, snowy fields. That's where the Snow Queen lives in her summer tent, but in winter her castle is in Finnmark, near the North Pole."

"Oh, Kay, dear Kay," said Gerda. And the robber girl said, "Keep still, or I'll knife you."

But in the morning, when Gerda told her the wood-pigeons' tale, she looked thoughtful, and asked the reindeer, "Do you know where Lapland is?"

"No one knows better," he said. "I was born and bred there, and galloped free over those plains of snow."

"Listen," the robber girl told Gerda. "The robber men have gone out, there's only my mother here, and at noon she will drink from a big bottle. After that she always takes a nap. That's when I will do you a good turn."

Sure enough, at noon the mother drank from the big bottle and fell asleep. Then the little robber girl told the reindeer, "I'd like to tickle you with my knife a little more, but never mind: I'm going to untie your rope and set you free to run away to Lapland, but you must take this little girl with you, and help her to find the Snow Queen and her friend Kay – I know you overheard us talking."

The reindeer jumped for joy. The robber girl picked Gerda up, put her on his back, and tied her in place, sitting on a little cushion.

"You can have your fur boots back," she said, "but I like your muff so much that I'm keeping it. Here are my mother's big mittens instead to keep your hands warm."

Gerda wept hot tears, and the little robber girl said, "Stop crying – aren't you happy now? Well, here are two loaves and a ham, so you won't starve."

Then she cut the reindeer's rope, and told him, "Run away, and take care of little Gerda."

Gerda waved goodbye to the little robber girl, and the reindeer ran away, carrying her over sticks and over stones, over woods and over plains, as fast as he could go. Wolves howled, ravens screeched, and red fire flashed in the sky. "See my friends the Northern Lights," said the reindeer, running even faster.

And by the time they reached Lapland, the loaves and the ham were all eaten.

THE LAPP WOMAN
AND THE FINN WOMAN

They stopped at a little hut with a very low doorway, and no one was at home except an old Lapp woman cooking fish over a whale-oil light. The reindeer told her their story, because Gerda was too cold to speak.

"You poor things," said the Lapp woman. "You still have hundreds of miles to go to reach Finnmark, where the Snow Queen is staying now. I have no paper, but I'll write the Finn woman a letter on a dried codfish. She will know more than I do."

So when Gerda was a little warmer, and had had some food and drink, the Lapp woman wrote a note on a dried fish and told her to look after it. Then she tied her on the reindeer again, and off they went, with the lovely Northern Lights, blue this time, flashing in the sky overhead.

Then at last they reached Finnmark and knocked on the Finn woman's chimney, because her hut had no door. It was very hot inside the hut, and the Finn woman, who looked small and dirty, wore few clothes. But she helped Gerda out of her mittens and boots, put some ice on the reindeer's head, and read the note written on the dried codfish. After reading it three times she knew what it said by heart, so she put the dried fish in her soup kettle. Waste not, want not – that was the Finn woman's motto. The reindeer told her his own story, and then Gerda's. "I know," he went on, "how wise you are. I know that you can tie up the winds of the world with knots in a piece of twine. If a sailor unties one knot he will have a fair wind, another and it's a strong gale, but the third and fourth will unloose a tempest that uproots trees. Can you brew this little girl a potion to give her the strength of twelve men so that she can defeat the Snow Queen?"

"The strength of twelve men? That wouldn't do her much good," said the Finn woman. Then she unfurled a parchment scroll with strange lettering on it, and read it to herself.

Once again the reindeer asked her to help Gerda, and then she took him aside, and told him, in a whisper, "Yes, little Kay is with the Snow Queen, and because he has a splinter of the devil's mirror in his heart and a speck of it in his eye, he won't be free of their evil power or of the Snow Queen until they are gone. But I can't give Gerda more strength than she already has through her own pure innocence. She will have to make Kay human again by herself.

"So take her to the Snow Queen's garden, leave her by the bush of red berries, and come back here at once. Off you go!"

So saying, she lifted Gerda back on the reindeer, forgetting about her boots and mittens, and away they went.

When they reached the bush of berries, the reindeer put Gerda down and ran back.

There stood Gerda, freezing cold, in the icy country of Finnmark. She had just begun running when snowflakes swirled around her – but they didn't fall from the clear sky where the Northern Lights shone. They skittered over the ground, growing larger all the time.

Gerda remembered looking at snowflakes under Kay's magnifying glass, but here they looked much worse, like strange monsters, and they were the Snow Queen's guard.

They were ugly, distorted, and twisted, but all of them were white – because they were snowflakes.

When Gerda, frightened, said the Lord's Prayer, the exhalation of her own breath froze as it came out of her mouth.

As the mist grew denser, shapes formed
in it - little angels wearing helmets,
and carrying shields and spears.
More and more of them appeared,
and when Gerda had finished
saying her prayer she had a legion
of angels around her.
They fought and conquered the ugly snowflakes, leaving them
in fragments one by one, and when they had rubbed Gerda's
hands and feet warm, she went on without fear to the Snow
Queen's palace.

Seventh Story IN THE SNOW QUEEN'S PALACE

But what had been happening to Kay all this time? To tell you the truth, he hadn't thought of Gerda at all, and had no idea that she was so close to the Snow Queen's palace. Its walls were made of driven snow, and the wind's sharp blade cut doors and windows in them. The palace had more than a hundred rooms, huge and empty, icy and glittering, illuminated by the Northern Lights, and there was no fun in any of them - no games or laughter. In the middle of the main hall there was a frozen lake, broken into many fragments of ice that could be arranged to form shapes, like a puzzle, and when the Snow Queen was in her palace she called it the Mirror of Reason.

But she was away just now, flying south to look at the warm countries, and the volcanoes of Etna and Vesuvius. Only Kay sat in the great hall. He was blue with cold, almost black, but he didn't feel it, because the Snow Queen had kissed the cold away. He was trying to make words out of the puzzle pieces, one word in particular. It was "Eternity," and if he could spell it out with the ice, the Queen had said, "You'll be your own master, and I'll give you the whole world and a new pair of skates."

Yet however hard he tried, he couldn't solve the puzzle. He just sat there, frozen stiff, and that was how Gerda found him when she walked into the palace. She recognized him at once, and flung her arms around him.

"Kay, dear Kay," she cried. "At long, long last I've found you!"

But Kay still sat there, frozen stiff. Then Gerda burst into hot tears. They fell on him, and when they touched his heart they melted the splinter of glass in it. He looked at Gerda, and she sang the lines from their childhood psalm:

> *Roses wither where they lie,*
> *But God's dear love will never die.*

Now it was Kay who burst out crying. His tears washed the other glass splinter away – the one in his eye – and he remembered his happy childhood with Gerda. "Oh, where have you been all this time?" he asked. "And where have I been, where are we now? This place is so huge and empty, and so cold!"

The two of them laughed and cried for joy, clinging to one another. Their happiness made even the frozen fragments of the puzzle dance about, and they formed the word "Eternity" of their own accord. So now Kay was free of the Snow Queen. He had solved her puzzle, he had won the world and a new pair of skates, and his new-found happiness brought the color back into his cheeks.

The two of them left the great, cold palace, still talking about their happy past in the garden on the roof, Gerda's grandmother and the tales she told.

As they went on, the bitter wind died down, the sun came out, and when they came to the bush that bore red berries, the kind reindeer was waiting there. He had brought a young female reindeer with him. She gave them her warm milk to drink, and they all went on together to the Finn woman's hot little hut. She told them how to reach the Lapp woman, who had made new clothes for them and put her sleigh in order. With the two reindeer running beside the sleigh, they reached the frontiers of the north country, and found green buds on the bushes. They said goodbye to the Lapp woman and the reindeer, and continued on foot. Soon they saw a girl riding through the springtime woods on a fine horse – the horse that had once drawn the golden carriage. Gerda recognized the little robber girl at once. She was off to seek her fortune in the north country, with two pistols stuck in her belt and a red cap on her head.

"So was it worth Gerda's while to go to the ends of the earth for you?" the robber girl asked Kay. But Gerda told her the whole story, and they all parted as friends.

They shook hands, and the little robber girl rode away. Kay and Gerda walked on, holding hands, through lovely spring weather. Soon they saw the towers of the city where they used to live. They walked into their old street, up the stairs and into Grandmother's room. Everything was the same as ever, with the clock going tick-tock, except for one thing: they saw that they were not children any more, but a man and woman grown – though with the innocent hearts of children. The roses in the roof garden were in flower, and as Kay and Gerda sat in the sunshine with Grandmother they forgot all about the Snow Queen and her cold palace. They sang the old psalm:

> *Roses wither where they lie,*
> *But God's dear love will never die.*

And now it was a warm, beautiful summer, and they lived happily ever after.